Sleeping Beauty

Once upon a time
there lived a king and queen and
they had a beautiful daughter.
They were so happy when she was born
that they had a great feast and
invited all the good fairies in the land.

Every fairy brought a present
for the beautiful princess and
the king gave every fairy
a gold box with jewels inside.

Now there was one wicked fairy
who was not invited to the feast.
But she came all the same!
She was so angry that she said,
"If the princess pricks her finger
on a spindle she will die."

But one of the good fairies quickly said,
"No, she shall not die.
If she pricks her finger
on a spindle she shall sleep
for a hundred years
and she will only wake up
if a prince kisses her."

Well, the king did not want
his beautiful daughter to sleep
for a hundred years so he said,
"Burn all the spindles in the land.
No-one must spin with a spindle ever again."

By Royal Decree
All Spindles
To Be Burnt
In
This land

All went well until the princess
was sixteen years old.
Then one day she went into a room
right at the top of the castle.
There she found an old woman
spinning with a spindle.
"What are you doing?" said the princess.
"I am spinning," said the woman.
"Here, **you** have a try."

Well, the princess took the spindle and
almost at once she pricked her finger.
Then she fell fast asleep.
The old woman told the king and
the king sent for the good fairy.
The good fairy came and said,
"If the princess wakes up
she must see people she knows around her."

Then the good fairy took out her wand.
She touched the servants and
they fell asleep.
She touched the cooks and
they fell asleep.
She touched the guards and
they fell asleep.
She even touched the fire and
it fell asleep.

The king and queen left the castle and,
at once, a thick wood of bushes and thorns
grew up all around.

Now no-one could get in or out
of the castle.
And it stayed like that
for years and years and years.

A hundred years later
a prince was out hunting and
he came to the thick wood
of bushes and thorns.

"What is inside the thick wood?"
said the prince to an old man.
Then the old man told him all about
the beautiful sleeping princess.

When the prince heard this
he wanted to see the princess for himself.
So he rode up to the wood
and the bushes and thorns bent back
to let him through.
Soon he came to the castle.
He passed the sleeping guards.
He saw the sleeping cooks and
the sleeping servants.

At last the prince came to the room
where the princess was asleep.
At once he fell in love with her and
he bent down and kissed her.
She opened her eyes, yawned,
stretched out her arms and woke up!

Then the servants woke up,
the cooks woke up,
the guards woke up and
the fire started to burn again.
Everyone was hungry so
the cooks made a great feast.

Well, the princess fell in love
with the prince and soon
they were married.
The prince stayed for a few days
and then he went home.

The prince did not tell his father
or his mother about the wedding.
His mother was really a wicked witch
and the prince was afraid of her.

For two years the prince went
to see his beautiful wife and
they had two children,
a girl called Morning and
a boy called Day.

Then, one day the old king died and
the prince became the new king.
He rode off to his wife and said,
"Now I am king you must come
to live with me in my palace."

So the beautiful princess went to live
in the palace with her children.
They were all very happy, but
that is not the end of the story.

Soon there was a war and
the new king had to go away
to lead his army.
Now the wicked queen hated
the princess and her children.
One day she said to her servant,
"Go and kill Morning.
Cook her and bring her to me
so that I can eat her up!"

But the servant would not kill
the little girl.
He hid her in his house and
killed a lamb instead.
The wicked queen ate the lamb but
she thought it was Morning.

Next day the wicked queen
sent for her servant and said,
"Go and kill Day.
Cook him and bring him to me!"

But the servant would not kill
the little boy.
He hid him in his house and
killed a goat instead.
The wicked queen ate the goat but
she thought it was Day.

Next day the wicked queen said,
"Go and kill the princess.
Cook her and bring her to me
so that I can eat her up!"

Again the servant would not do it,
so he hid the princess in his house and
killed a deer instead.
The wicked queen ate the deer but
she thought it was the princess.

But one day the wicked queen went past
her servant's house and saw
Morning, Day and the princess.

She was very angry.
She filled a big tub with poisonous snakes.
Then she tied up her servant,
Morning, Day and the princess.
But just as she was about to throw them all
into the tub, the king came back from war.

The wicked queen was so afraid
of what the king would do
that she jumped into the tub and
the snakes killed her at once.

So that was the end
of the wicked queen
and this is the end
of the story.